CHARLIE
The
Lonesome
Cougar

CHARLIE
The
Lonesome
Cougar

by Mark Van Cleefe

Based on the Walt Disney screenplay
by Jack Speirs

Story by Jack Speirs and Winston Hibler

Illustrated by Bob Cassell

SCHOLASTIC BOOK SERVICES

NEW YORK • LONDON • RICHMOND HILL, ONTARIO

Based on the screenplay by Jack Speirs
Story by Jack Speirs and Winston Hibler

A hardcover edition of this book is published by Four
Winds Press, a division of Scholastic, and is avail-
able through your local bookstore or directly from
Four Winds Press, 50 West 44th St., N.Y., N.Y. 10036.

1st printing...April 1968
Printed in the U.S.A.

CONTENTS

JESS TAKES A ROOMMATE

THE day Jess Bradley found the baby cougar, he was deep inside the Cascade Mountains on the Montana-Wyoming border.

Jess was a tall, rangy young man in his twenties who had always had a love of the woods. In his present job as an industrial forester, he marked trees just ahead of a logging crew of the Carbon County Lumber Company. He went from tree to tree, spraying a large yellow "C" on healthy pines he selected for lumber.

On this particular day Jess's paint spray can was hissing regularly in the silence of the forest when gradually Jess became conscious of an unfamiliar sound, a faint cry coming from behind a windfall pine. Guided by the cry, he cautiously searched along the ground and there, sprawled near the roots of the fallen tree, lay a baby cougar.

7

Jess was not too surprised to come across a cougar in these parts; the Pacific Northwest was well populated with this breed of cat. Nevertheless, he'd never seen a cub before and had only glimpsed the elusive adult cougar a few times in the past. His curiosity was aroused.

He put down his sprayer, knelt beside the kitten, and looked it over, not touching it. Its eyes were not yet open, and the only signs of life were its thin mewing and an occasional twitch of its little legs.

Jess had a college degree in forestry and had also learned woodsmanship firsthand and he knew something was wrong. Why was this kitten outside the den before its eyes were even open? A mother cougar would never allow that. Jess lightly examined the kitten all over. It was nothing but skin and bones — obviously it hadn't been fed for two or three days.

Something's wrong all right, Jess thought. The female cougar is a devoted mother; if she hadn't returned by now, it could mean only one thing — she never would. A bounty hunter had killed her, most likely. There have been bounties on the cougar for more than a hundred years because of its natural tendency to kill livestock and deer, its chief source of food.

Jess lifted the unprotesting kitten and stood up. As he gently stroked its soft fur he looked down the slope thoughtfully. It was plain this little cat wouldn't last another day without food. He looked down at it; it nuzzled his chest, found a braided-leather button on Jess's jacket and began sucking at it. Jess shook his head, smiled, and made up his mind.

"Well, now," he said, "I guess I can put up with you if you can put up with me." At that moment Jess didn't have any idea about the "putting up" he'd have to do.

He picked up his spray can and headed down the hill for home with his new — a bit unusual — room-mate: an orphaned cougar!

GOOD-TIME CHARLIE

As Jess pulled up in front of his house the sun was just going down behind the mountain peaks. He jumped down from the pickup and reached for the dozing cougar kitten. It awoke and began to cry at the top of its voice.

Jess tucked the kitten under his jacket and waited for it to quiet down. Leaning against the open door of the truck, he gazed out toward the mountains. Their snowy peaks were turning pink in the sunset. Below the snowline, the slopes were splotched with the light green of newly leafed trees among the darker evergreens. The sweet freshness of the air, too, spoke of spring. This was the time of year that Jess liked best. His snug cabin overlooking a hidden mountain lake seemed to him the best place in the world. He was usually too busy to be lonely.

There was a sudden squirming and mewing inside his jacket. Jess shook himself from his reverie and grinned.

"Okay, okay!" he said. "I get the message."

He picked up a brown paper bag from the floor of the truck, and shut the door. As he walked toward the house the mewing kitten stuck his head out and moved about blindly. Jess held the bag up, as if the kitten could see it.

"Lucky for you Mrs. Burns was still at the store and had a bottle nipple, fella. Otherwise, you might've had to wait till morning!"

Dawn was breaking as Jess looked at the clock. He groaned and looked at the baby cougar in his arms, nursing away at a soda pop bottle full of milk.

"It's five o'clock in the morning, you crazy cat! You're just going to have to get yourself on another schedule!" This was the first time — but not the last — that Jess wondered if adopting a cougar was such a good idea.

Minutes later, after the kitten had finished drinking and fallen asleep in his arms, Jess set it gently down on a blanket on the floor next to his dresser. He looked longingly at his bed and shrugged. There was no use in going to bed now. He'd only have to get up again in an hour. Cautiously he opened the bottom drawer of his dresser, pulled out some clean clothes, and went into the bathroom to shower.

At the sound of the rushing water, the kitten woke up, bobbed its head around in the air, and bumped into the open dresser drawer. With its two front paws on the edge of the drawer, it managed to pull itself up by scratching frantically with its hind legs and promptly toppled head first into the drawer.

When Jess came out of the bathroom, the kitten was missing from the blanket. Jess hastily searched all around. The scratches on his dresser led him to the kitten. In the corner of his dresser drawer lay a ball of spotted fur, snuggled into a pile of soft, woolly socks.

After three weeks of care and feeding, Jess's cougar kitten had really filled out. It weighed about seven pounds and had grown to nearly sixteen inches in length. Jess figured it to be about five weeks old. In another week he would start it on solid foods.

Yes, the kitten was full of good health, all right — and full of good old-fashioned kitten mischief, too. From the moment it had opened its eyes, it couldn't wait to investigate every nook and cranny of Jess's four-room house. And like any cat, it was particularly intrigued by anything that dangled.

One day while Jess was working at home on the logging report, the only part of his job he didn't particularly like, the baby cougar was playing on the back of the couch, next to Jess's desk. As Jess lifted a bottle of soda he struck the end of the light chain on his desk lamp. It began to sway back and forth. The moving chain completely entranced the kitten. Its eyes moved back and forth, following the swinging chain as it tensed for the attack. Crouching low, it began slowly edging toward the chain.

Jess was frowning down at the papers before him when suddenly, right in the middle of everything, landed the kitten — kerplunk!

Jess quickly shoved back from the desk.

"Hey!" he shouted, just as the soda ran all over his

papers and began dripping on him. He jumped up, bumping the edge of the desk. Down went a copper tumbler filled with pencils, the kitten right after them. Just as the kitten began a fresh attack on the rolling pencils, it felt itself lifted off the floor by a very disgusted Jess.

"Now, you look here," Jess said, heading for the front door. "I'm trying to work, and you're always making like a Good Time Charlie." Jess opened the door and set the kitten down outside. "You know, I think I'll just name you that. Call you Charlie for short. Now, go on outside to have your good time, Charlie!" And he shut the door.

Jess figured that young Charlie was too small to go very far and not likely to get into trouble close by. But Charlie was a cougar that was born either to find trouble or make it and he just couldn't wait to get started!

OUT ON A LIMB

CHARLIE stood in the grass and surveyed the great outdoors for the first time. A brown wind-blown leaf skipped under his nose, and he immediately pounced on it. But it crumbled in no time, so Charlie looked for other diversions. He sniffed at a white-topped dandelion, shook his head, and sneezed as the fuzz tickled his nose. He bounded down a shallow hill and came to a sudden halt. There on a boulder sat a marmot, a funny little short-legged animal of the rodent family. Charlie stood very still, his head to the side, not knowing what to make of it. The marmot spotted Charlie, whistled, and scampered behind the boulder. He took a dim view of all cougars, big or little, wild or tame.

Charlie had never played hide and seek before. He bumble-footed over and peeked around the boulder. Something stirred behind him. Charlie darted in the di-

15

rection of the sound and discovered a hole in the ground. Charlie looked at it, sniffed it, then poked an exploring paw down into the hole. The hole suddenly seemed to explode! A deluge of dirt showered up into Charlie's face, followed by the rear view of an irate badger. Charlie stumbled backward, and the badger turned and faced him, growling indignantly. That sent Charlie flying back up the hill.

Here, after a few uneasy moments, Charlie again sat down on the grass. He took a few swipes at some swaying weeds, chased his tail, walked a narrow log.

Then down by the lake something moved. Charlie padded on down, and, sure enough, there was a little furry-tailed, reddish-brown fellow, chattering away and scampering along the shore.

Charlie played follow-the-leader. Wherever the squirrel went, Charlie ran right behind him. No doubt the squirrel figured he was being chased, not followed. He made a hurried dash up the nearest tree, which was leaning out over the water.

Charlie followed to the base of the tree. As soon as he saw the squirrel chattering furiously on a branch, Charlie waited no longer. He scrambled up the sloping trunk of the tree. Meanwhile the squirrel ran to the tip of the limb and leaped across to another tree.

Charlie followed, easing himself out on to the limb. The limb grew narrower and narrower, and Charlie soon found he could go no farther. He then tried going backward, but he lost his footing, slipped, and landed straddle-legged on the limb. He dug his claws in for dear life and took stock of his situation. He was hopelessly trapped.

There was only one thing for a kitten to do. Charlie let out a few trial mews. Then they grew into ear-splitting, wailing squalls.

Jess came running out of the house and hurried down the hill to the lake. He located Charlie without any trouble. Looking up at Charlie, he put his hands on his hips and grinned.

"Hang on, Charlie. I'll get you down — if you'll shut up."

Jess started to shinny up the tree. Charlie quieted down and watched intently.

"Just take it easy, cat," Jess said. "Everything is under control."

Jess eased himself out on a branch just beneath Charlie. But Charlie couldn't wait to be rescued. He tried to move backward to meet Jess, and just as Jess looked up, Charlie began to slip.

"No, Charlie!" Jess cried. "No — stay there — don't — ! No!"

Charlie let go and landed sprawling and clawing, on the top of Jess's head. The overloaded limb split under the sudden impact, and Jess and Charlie, both yelling, dropped right through the branches and plummeted into the lake.

When Jess came up, sputtering and shaking his head, he found Charlie right behind him, drenched but unruffled. As a matter of fact, the crazy cat was downright enjoying himself!

Jess tried to look angry.

"Nice going, Tarzan," he said and exploded with laughter.

CHARLIE MEETS CHAINSAW

THE Carbon County Lumber Mill was headquarters for Jess. He spent a good part of his time working there in the office. On these days he had taken to hauling Charlie around with him. By the time Charlie was six months old, he had quite a circle of friends at the mill.

Charlie had developed into a beautiful tawny mountain lion. His black baby spots had faded almost completely; the muscles in his shoulders were growing strong. He weighed over forty pounds.

Jess pulled up alongside the Mill Cafe, opened the door on the passenger side of the truck, and Charlie bounded down. He headed toward the kitchen door.

"Hey, Potlatch," Jess called through the screen door, "you've got company!"

Potlatch was the owner and cook of the cafe. He was a happy-go-lucky fellow who could rustle up a meal

in short order for the hungry men at the mill. At the moment he was molding hamburger patties at the kitchen table. When Jess called he turned around and grinned.

"So I see," he called back.

Charlie reached the door and sat down. This was a special game Charlie played with Potlatch. Charlie would sit patiently at the back door, staring and sniffing. The next move was Potlatch's. Potlatch took a heaping handful of hamburger and slapped it into a pie tin. Then he carried it outside to Charlie.

Jess chuckled. "Poor ol' Charlie. He only had two pounds of liver this morning." Jess put the truck into gear. "Well, I'll be over at the office, in case my cat here faints from starvation."

Potlatch laughed. "Okay. See you later, Jess."

Jess drove off toward the mill office, about fifty yards away. Potlatch, holding the pan of meat, looked down at Charlie.

"Mornin', Charlie," he said. "How about a smile before breakfast, huh?"

Charlie bared his fangs and gave Potlatch his very best smile.

"Very good, fella," returned Potlatch. He patted Charlie on the head and put the food before him. "Got a little surprise I picked up last night," he continued. "Just wait."

Potlatch disappeared into the kitchen, and Charlie began to eat. Potlatch came back, carrying a black and white puppy. Charlie stopped eating to look up with interest.

"Here's a little playmate for you, Charlie," Potlatch said, putting the puppy down. "Chainsaw, say hello."

21

Chainsaw exploded into a fury of yaps and yowls and moved in on the food pan. Charlie leaped backward and cocked his head to the side, looking puzzled. Chainsaw stood guard over the pan of food, a low growl rumbling inside of him. Charlie tried to sneak up to the food, edging very carefully toward it. But Chainsaw erupted again, and Charlie stopped dead in his tracks.

Potlatch reached down and picked up the puppy.

"You're just plain askin' for trouble, pup. Don't you know a mountain lion when you see one?"

Charlie, now that the dog was being held, approached the food pan with the intention of polishing off his meat. But Chainsaw went wild. With a great burst of yelps, he jerked loose from Potlatch's grip and bolted toward Charlie. Charlie spun around and took off in the direction of the mill office, Chainsaw yapping at his heels.

Potlatch yelled, "Chainsaw, stop that — come back here!" He ran after the pup.

Jess and the mill manager were standing in the mill office in front of a township map, which hung on the wall.

"Section 39, here," Jess was saying as he pointed to the map, "is ready to log right now. There is about — "

He was interrupted by a torrent of barks and yelps. He and the manager stepped to the window to see what was up.

Charlie whizzed past, followed by the yapping Chainsaw. Potlatch, yelling at the puppy, brought up the rear. In three elastic bounds, Charlie landed on the hood of Jess's pickup. Chainsaw pulled up alongside the truck, barking shrilly. Finally Potlatch, panting and out of breath, grabbed the puppy and gave him a swat.

"What kinda way is that to act, you?" Picking up the struggling pup, he headed back toward the cafe.

Jess watched him, shook his head, and grinned at the mill manager.

"Mighty fierce animal, a cougar," he said.

The manager smiled too, but he was a bit doubtful.

"He's still a youngster," he replied, "but he'll grow up someday. He could change, you know, Jess."

Jess looked out at Charlie, asleep on the top of the pickup. He smiled fondly at his cougar. "Oh, I don't think Charlie will ever be a problem."

THE COUGAR
IS A PREDATORY ANIMAL

CHARLIE and Jess liked to go fishing. That is, Jess liked fishing. While he fished, Charlie usually watched him or went exploring.

One fine spring morning, a year after Jess had found the cougar, Charlie was stretched across a boulder while Jess cast his line into the water. Charlie was now a good-sized cat — weighing nearly seventy pounds and measuring five feet in length. But he was still a youngster and only half the size of a grown cougar.

When Jess swung the line around to cast, Charlie lifted his head with interest. He jumped down from the rock and bounded over to the water's edge.

Jess was standing in the water, which reached midway up his boots. Charlie splashed up behind him. Jess completed his casting, then turned to Charlie and gave him an affectionate swat.

"Shhh," he said. "You want to scare them away? We've only caught one all afternoon."

Charlie batted a paw at Jess's feet, then bumped against his legs.

Jess grinned. "Oh, yeah. You're a real mean lion, you are." He turned away to keep watch on his fishing line, ignoring the cougar.

Charlie ambled along the edge of the water to a point where the woods grew to the lake. Then he moved off through the trees. Almost instantly he saw an otter playing in the pine needles.

Charlie crouched low and froze. The stalking instinct is strong in any cougar, but Charlie used it strictly for fun. And to a playful creature like the otter, almost anything seemed to be for fun.

The chase was on.

Charlie and the otter flashed through the trees. Over and under fallen logs they ran. Finally the otter headed out of the woods along the open shoreline.

Jess looked up as he was putting another fish into his creel.

"Charlie?" he said, looking around.

Then he saw them, barreling toward him. The otter ran in zigzag movements along the water's edge, Charlie bounding right behind him.

Jess dropped his flyrod and creel on the bank.

"Charlie!" Jess yelled. "Cut it out, Charlie. Stop that!"

The otter saw Jess running toward them. It swerved, jumped onto a log lodged in the shallows of the lake, and slithered under the water.

Charlie followed, running to the very end of the log.

There he halted. He peered with puzzlement at the rings of water where the otter had disappeared.

Slowly the log began to drift away from shore with Charlie on it.

"Hey!" Jess called.

He dashed into the water after the floating log and found himself waist deep in a hole.

Charlie looked over at Jess. Jess glared at him. Then Charlie jumped into the lake and waded to shore on his own.

Jess climbed out, muddy water spilling out of his boots and dripping from his clothes. He shook his fist at Charlie.

"Why don't you grow up, huh?"

Charlie cocked his head to the side, listening.

"The next time I catch you chasin' critters around here," Jess said sternly, "I'll tan your hide — with you in it!"

Charlie sat innocently looking at Jess. He recognized that tone of voice. He knew it meant business.

"Come along now, Charlie. And stay close."

Charlie "heeled" behind Jess. When they'd gone a few paces back toward the fishing spot, Jess stopped suddenly and pointed ahead.

"Hey!" he said. "Look at that durn otter!"

It was all Charlie could do to stay put. And this time he would have done better to chase his old playmate. The otter had his head stuck right in Jess's fishing creel.

"Get out of there!" Jess shouted.

But the otter paid no heed this time to the running, shouting Jess. He pulled a trout from the creel, raced to the shoreline, slipped into the water, and disappeared again.

Jess stopped running and Charlie came loping up beside him.

"Charlie," he said, "I caught two fish, one for you and one for me." He pointed at the water, still rippling from the otter's hasty retreat. "There went yours."

The adventure with the otter raised a question in Jess's mind. The cougar is a predatory animal. It stalks and kills its food. Roaming the countryside like a phantom plunderer, the cougar was once considered the leading predator of North America. As white men brought in livestock, however, the cougar was hunted out of existence in most parts of the country. From a few last strongholds, mostly in the mountains, the cougar of the wilds still comes out to stalk his prey. And his prey is usually deer.

It wasn't long before Jess was to learn the answer to his question: Just how strong was Charlie's hunting instinct?

One day Jess was making a timber survey in the woods. It was a clear, sunny autumn afternoon and Charlie was along. Everywhere there was a profusion of red, orange, gold, and pink brush nestled among the evergreens.

Jess stopped in an open area to set up his surveyor's transit and tripod. Charlie watched him for a moment, then strolled off toward a clump of underbrush. He stopped, sniffed along the ground, and began to stalk toward a bush.

Jess, his equipment now set up, watched him

thoughtfully. As Charlie crept closer to the bush Jess stepped up behind him, squinted against the sun, and saw a fawn raise its head alertly. It stared up at Jess with big, frightened eyes, then broke from the brush. Charlie uncoiled and bounded after it.

"Charlie, stop it! Come here, Charlie!" Jess ran after him, but both the animals disappeared into the woods.

Jess charged through the dense underbrush, stumbling and calling his pet. He was very much afraid of what he would find when he caught up. When he reached a clearing, he stopped, gasping for breath.

There was Charlie with the fawn trapped between his big paws. But there was no bloody murder. Charlie was washing the terrified little deer with his tongue!

Jess stood there, shaking his head.

"Charlie, Charlie," he said, "one of us has an awful lot to learn about cougars."

He went over and knelt beside the two animals. Carefully he took Charlie by the scruff of his neck, pulled him back, and held him.

"Go on home, little fella," Jess said to the fawn. He gave it a shove, and the fawn darted off into the woods. Jess watched the fawn until it disappeared from view. Then he released Charlie, who stayed beside him, licking his hand.

"Charlie," said Jess, "you're no more dangerous than a kitten!" But Jess knew that kittens have a disturbing habit of growing up into cats. . . .

CRUISING DOWN THE RIVER

THE annual log drive was under way, and Jess and Charlie were in the midst of it. Jess was glad to be out of doors every day. So was Charlie.

The logging site was an exciting place to be. The noise of chainsaws filled the air. Workers were climbing trees. Others were hammering wedges into trees. There was an occasional "Timber!" as a tall pine toppled to the ground. Trucks and trainloads of logs were being hauled out of the woods. Then they were dumped into feeder streams to float down to the Big Carbon River.

Arriving one morning with Charlie, Jess climbed out of the truck.

"Hold on, Charlie," said Jess. "You'll have to sit this one out."

Charlie looked at him curiously, but backed up and stayed put. Jess reached behind the seat and pulled out a rolled-up map. He tapped Charlie on the nose and smiled. "Be a good boy, now," he said. Shutting the door, he walked away.

At least Charlie had a good view of all the hustle-bustle outside. In the midst of all the goings-on, he saw the familiar figure of his old friend, Potlatch. Potlatch was carrying a carton down the bank of the nearest stream toward the kitchen barge or "wanigan." Cases of food were piled high on the deck of the floating wanigan. The hard-working rivermen ate a lot as they drove the logs downstream. At this moment Jess arrived with the river boss, Mac.

"Man, look at that cat!" Mac said. "Hi ya, Charlie, long time no see!"

Charlie bared his fangs in his special grin. Mac and Jess laughed. "Well, Jess," Mac said, "we'll see you in a couple of weeks." The men shook hands, and Mac headed down the bank. The big wanigan was ready to move out.

Jess climbed up into the driver's seat, backed his truck, and turned around. As he started to pull away, he saw Potlatch lifting a heavy carton.

"I'd better give our pal a hand, Charlie. Wouldn't want to see anything happen to your best meal ticket, would you?" Jess said.

He drove his pickup slowly among the trucks and buses and cars parked along the river bank. At last he pulled up alongside Potlatch's panel truck.

"Well, look who's here!" Jess grinned, as Chainsaw leaped across the seat of the panel truck, barking. Chainsaw was bigger, but not a bit better-tempered.

Jess leaned over and rolled up the window next to

Charlie, leaving only a small space for fresh air.

"Sorry, Charlie," he apologized. "It wouldn't do to have a frolicking cougar loose around here." "Anyway," he added, stepping out of the truck, "you'd just go get yourself dog-bit."

Jess closed the door. Chainsaw, barking and yapping, was leaning halfway out of his window. Charlie slumped down in the driver's seat of Jess's truck.

"Why don't you pipe down, Chainsaw?" Jess said and joined Potlatch.

"Hey!" a loud voice roared over Chainsaw's barking a moment later. "Somebody get that pickup out of the way."

Charlie turned to look at a big red-faced man behind the wheel of a bus. Jess's pickup blocked the way. The red-faced man stuck his head out of the bus.

"Hey, Charlie," he called. "Move your pal's truck!" Everybody laughed. Cars behind the bus were sounding their horns impatiently.

The bus driver edged out of his seat. The other fellows on the bus laughed and jeered.

"Look out for the ferocious animal."

"Yeah, maybe old Charlie won't remember you no more."

"Get yourself a chair before you get in that lion's den, buddy."

The red-faced man ignored all the remarks. He was a little scared. Although he didn't realize it, there was reason for him to be *very* scared. Chainsaw's barking had frazzled poor Charlie's nerves.

The man spoke softly and soothingly as he approached the truck.

"Nice Charlie," he said. "Remember me, pal?" Cautiously he opened the door. Charlie sprang across the seat, leaped out, and dove under the truck. There he lay, crouched on the ground. Chainsaw spotted him, bolted out of the window and charged the big cat.

Charlie took off at top speed down the bank toward the stream. Potlatch, carrying the last of the food supplies, swerved to one side as Charlie passed him. But Chainsaw, in hot pursuit of Charlie, ran right into Potlatch. The dog, the carton of canned goods, and the man went rolling down the bank.

Jess had just handed over a carton to the drive cook when they both heard the commotion. The drive cook looked up, and terror crossed his face. As Jess spun around, Charlie flew over his head and landed on top of the kitchen wanigan.

"Charlie!" Jess bellowed.

The drive cook didn't know who "Charlie" was and didn't wait to find out. He dropped the food carton on the deck of the wanigan and sprang to shore, tripping on the mooring line and pulling it loose.

Jess called after the running cook, "Hey, come on back here! He won't hurt you! He — " But the cook was already up the bank, and there was no getting him back.

Now Jess had another problem on his hands. The wanigan, loosed from its mooring, was caught in the current. It was pulling rapidly away from shore. Grabbing the mooring line, Jess strained to keep it from letting out any farther.

Nearby, Potlatch stared with his mouth open — first at Jess, then out at the wanigan with Charlie crouched on top of a pile of boxes. He jumped to his feet.

"Hold it, Jess!" he shouted, running.

By now, the wanigan had drifted out thirty or forty feet. Potlatch ran up behind Jess, grabbed him around the waist, and the two men gave a great tug on the rope. The jolt knocked a stack of cartons off the opposite side of the barge — and Charlie with it! Charlie swam around in the middle of all the debris, then climbed up on a passing log.

Jess and Potlatch were still straining at the rope. Suddenly Chainsaw took off along the edge of the bank, barking wildly. The men looked downstream. There was Charlie, sitting on a log, drifting downriver.

Potlatch let go of Jess's waist and straightened up. "Well, I'll be — "

The rope snapped taut. Before Potlatch could grab him, Jess was yanked headlong into the river.

When Jess surfaced, he was in the same current with the wanigan. He pulled himself hand-over-hand along the rope until he reached the wanigan. Climbing aboard, he looked back at the shore. Potlatch was waving helplessly. Jess turned and squinted down the river. A good distance away and floating faster every minute, Charlie and his log drifted toward a bend in the river.

Jess ran along the deck to the outboard motor and yanked the starter cord. It came out. He looked at it with disgust and dropped it on the deck. Then he grabbed a long sweep oar and tried to get a little more speed out of the clumsy wanigan. Charlie disappeared around the bend.

"Well," said Jess to himself, "at least we're going in the same direction!"

34

On shore, Potlatch and the drive cook, who had come back down the bank, stood looking downriver.

Potlatch said, "You know, that river is halfway to the mill before it comes to another road. I sure hope Jess Bradley's a good cook!"

OUT OF THE WATER
INTO THE FRYING PAN

WHEN Jess finally caught sight of Charlie again, the cougar was already in a jam — a log jam! He was perched on top of a stack of logs that had become wedged against a boulder. When he saw Jess and the wanigan coming toward him, Charlie started wailing.

But the runaway wanigan was caught in a powerful current. Jess worked the oar furiously but in vain. He drifted past Charlie, about twenty feet away. All he could do was yell a few encouraging words.

"Stay right there, Charlie. Don't go away. I'll be back — don't worry, boy!"

As Jess drifted out of sight around the next bend, Charlie looked mournfully after him.

Some distance downstream from Jess and Charlie, the big bunkhouse wanigan was moored to the shore. Mac, the river boss, who had just driven down from the mill, stood on the deck discussing the drive with one of the workmen, Joe.

"You and some of the boys can go back up and clear that big center jam first thing in the morning," Mac said.

"All right, and there's a little tie-up just below it, in the eddy — "

Joe was interrupted by Mac.

"Look there!" Mac said, pointing upriver. "That crazy cook is all alone on that kitchen wanigan. He's trying to *row* it!"

"Maybe he broke a propeller," Joe said.

"Better get some help and give him a hand," Mac ordered.

"Right."

Joe motioned to the driver of a nearby motorboat. Quickly he jumped aboard and soon pulled up alongside the kitchen wanigan where Jess was stranded.

"Why, it's Jess Bradley!" Joe said, surprised. "What happened, Jess?"

"Give me a hand," said Jess. "Let's tie this crazy wanigan to your boat."

They towed the kitchen wanigan to shore, and maneuvered it behind the big bunkhouse wanigan. Mac crossed the deck and saw Jess and Joe waving their arms in the air, arguing.

"Hey!" Mac shouted. "What's going on? What the heck you doing here, Jess Bradley?"

"I'm trying to get some help outta this guy," Jess said irritably.

Joe laughed. "You oughta hear this, boss. It's a great story."

Mac looked around the wanigan. "Never mind the story. Where's the cook?"

"The cook?" Jess looked blank. "Oh, he got left behind, but — "

"He *what?*" Mac exploded. "Look, I've got about forty hungry men to feed — "

"Now don't worry about the cook, he's all right. But Charlie's in trouble."

"Charlie?" Mac said. "I just saw him up at the logging site!"

"Yeah," Jess nodded, "but he's not there now. He's about ten miles upstream, sitting on a log jam!"

"Oh, no he ain't," said Joe, pointing. "There he is now!"

Jess and Mac turned around. Sure enough, there was Charlie, drifting on a log.

Jess grinned. "Well, look at that! He got loose from the jam! C'mon, Joe, let's get him."

Mac said, "No you don't, Joe."

Jess turned to Mac. "Whattaya mean, no? C'mon, Mac, give me a boat!"

Mac put his hands on his hips and shook his head. "Nope."

"But I've gotta get Charlie!"

Mac smiled. "And I've gotta get a cook."

"What are you talking about? I'm no cook, I'm a — "

Mac didn't budge. "No cook, no cougar," he said.

Jess looked downriver. Charlie was in midstream, floating away fast.

"I'm a cook!" Jess said desperately. "Now let's go get Charlie."

"We'll get Charlie," Mac grinned. "*You* start peeling spuds."

When the men got back with Charlie, Jess was seated on a stool, peeling the first of a mountainous pile of potatoes.

"Here's your cat, cookie," Joe called from the rescue boat. He gave Charlie a swat, and Charlie leaped aboard the kitchen wanigan.

Charlie padded over to Jess and sat down next to him.

"Thank you, too, buddy," Jess said.

Charlie moved closer, put a hesitant paw upon Jess's foot, and gave him a big grin. Jess looked at him.

"What are you grinning about, you . . . you overgrown pussycat."

Charlie grinned again.

Jess dropped the potato and peeler on the table, reached over and put his arm around Charlie's neck.

"Boy, am I glad to see you, fella."

PLAYING WITH DYNAMITE

DURING the next few days Jess and Charlie established a routine. Jess worked at the cooking and dishwashing. Charlie enjoyed himself.

Charlie had lost no time in making friends with the rivermen. When they drove the logs downstream, they often took him along in the work boat. Charlie would sit in the bow, his paws up on the gunwale, grinning into the wind. Sometimes he would ride a log. To do this, he shifted his weight from side to side, while the log spun under him. It was great fun! Charlie didn't know that this was a sport that logmen have always enjoyed. Neither did he know that cougars usually dislike the water.

Back on the kitchen wanigan, Jess felt trapped. And he knew who'd trapped him! From where he stood at the sink, surrounded by great stacks of dirty dishes, he could see Charlie riding downstream in the breeze.

"Boy!" he thought. "Why didn't I just get myself a nice ordinary dog?"

The long drive went smoothly until one day when the logs tangled up in the kind of jam that rivermen hate most to see. Logs were piled up so high that the men couldn't see downstream. All available manpower couldn't break them up. There was only one thing to do — blast them loose with dynamite.

The bunkhouse wanigan and Jess's kitchen wanigan were moored upstream, well out of the blasting area. Jess was stretched out on his bunk, taking a nap.

But Charlie was wide awake and playful. Jumping ashore, he noticed the dangling mooring line that held the wanigan to shore. Charlie began to bat and tug at the line. Then he rolled over with all four legs in the air and kicked at it. Grabbing the end of the line in his mouth, he backed up, tugging hard.

Finally the rope came loose, and Charlie almost lost his teeth. Instantly the wanigan slipped away from shore. With a flying leap, Charlie just managed to clutch the foredeck with his front paws.

Jess slept peacefully on.

Downstream at the log jam, a workman had lighted the dynamite fuse. He sprang back across the logs to shore. Watching him, Mac and Joe suddenly spotted the kitchen wanigan. Round a bend it came, drifting straight for the log jam where the dynamite fuse sputtered! Everyone knew the dynamite was due to explode in less than five minutes — everyone, that is, but Jess and Charlie.

"Turn around quick!" yelled Mac to the driver of his boat.

42

"There's no time . . ." began Joe.

At that moment the wanigan crashed into the log jam.

Charlie was thrown right onto the logs. In the cabin, Jess was hurled from his bunk to the floor. When he finally realized that he was not safely moored to the shore, Jess sprang to his feet. Stumbling among the scattered pots and pans, he dashed out to the deck.

The first thing he saw was Charlie — balancing himself on the logs with a long string in his mouth. On the end of that string dangled a stack of dynamite.

"Charlie!" Jess gasped. "Drop it — *drop it*, boy!"

Charlie looked at Jess. With his jaws still clamped on the fuse, he stepped gingerly down onto another log, moving in the direction of the wanigan.

Jess tried to keep the panic out of his voice.

"Charlie," he said very sternly, "you put that down and get back here. *Right now!*"

Charlie let the dynamite drop onto the logs. He knew Jess meant business. He bounded obediently onto the deck of the wanigan. As soon as Charlie was on the deck, Jess pulled the starter cord gripped in his hand. For once the outboard motor started instantly.

No sooner had they pulled away than the dynamite exploded! Logs and water showered from the air.

Jess and Charlie dove into the cabin of the wanigan.

A moment later Mac and Joe pulled alongside. Rushing into the cabin, they found Jess sprawled on the floor, face down. Charlie was hunched next to him, looking strange and wide-eyed.

"Jess — you all right?" Mac asked anxiously.

43

Jess pushed himself up with his hands and slowly turned around. He was covered with eggs. They dripped from his face, from his hair, from his clothes. Disgust dripped from his voice.

"Yeah," he said. "Just fine."

BACK TO
THE PEACEFUL LIFE

SUMMER, fall, and winter followed in quiet succession. By the time Charlie reached his second birthday the next spring, he was a full-grown cougar. He was over seven feet long and weighed a hundred sixty pounds. Although he was not an exceptionally large mountain lion, he was a strikingly beautiful and graceful animal. He had a sleek tawny brown coat, a white belly, and dark reddish-brown tips on his ears and tail.

Jess's work was not always outdoors. There were long periods when he worked at the mill every day. And Charlie always went with him. Charlie had work of his own to do — especially at lunch time. And for the lunch period, Charlie had worked out a careful routine.

A short time before the noon whistle Charlie would start out. This first part of his routine was an appetizer run. He visited members of his wide circle of friends, who were just opening their lunch boxes. Each had a tidbit for him, along with a friendly greeting or an affectionate pat.

Then, with precision timing, he would arrive at Potlatch's cafe exactly as the noon whistle blew. This was always the high point of his daily excursion. The reward was great, but there was one small problem — Chainsaw.

One fine spring day as the noon whistle split the air, Charlie arrived at his usual station at Potlatch's kitchen door. Chainsaw was lying under a tree, gnawing at a large bone. The dog looked up from his bone as Charlie reached the doorway.

Just inside the door stood Potlatch, holding a large chunk of roast beef behind his back.

"Well, whattaya say, Charlie? Think I might have a little smile?" Charlie was happy to oblige with one of his widest grins.

Potlatch chuckled, opened the door, and tossed out the meat. He turned and went back to his work.

Charlie trotted toward the meat as it landed in the grass. But Chainsaw was quicker. In a flash Chainsaw reached the meat and stood over it, growling possessively. Charlie froze. He looked at the meat longingly. Slowly Charlie moved around Chainsaw. The dog pivoted, always facing Charlie. Suddenly Charlie made a dash toward Chainsaw's abandoned bone. Chainsaw exploded into vicious barks and rushed to defend his bone. But Charlie had only pretended to want that bone. The instant Chainsaw headed for his bone, Charlie leaped over him, grabbed the meat, and ran.

For a moment Chainsaw was so bewildered he

stopped barking. Then with an enraged yelp, he set out in hot pursuit of Charlie and the meat.

Potlatch heard the commotion and threw his hands up in the air in exasperation.

"Oh no!" he groaned. "That durn dog —"

He pushed through the kitchen door.

Charlie was running toward the mill pond, with Chainsaw close behind.

"Chainsaw!" Potlatch yelled. "Stop it, come back here!"

Chainsaw was losing ground rapidly. When he heard Potlatch calling, he gave up the chase. Charlie disappeared into the bushes.

Potlatch shook his finger in Chainsaw's face. "Some day, somewhere, somebody's gonna tell Charlie he's a cougar, and then, Chainsaw, your life won't be worth a red cent."

A few minutes later Charlie came out from the bushes. He settled himself on the bank above the mill pond and began washing his face.

Below, the mill workers were staging a little lunch-hour birling match. This was the sport of balancing on a spinning log in the river. The men would challenge each other to see who could stay up the longest.

Charlie watched the men intently, then padded on down to the edge of the pond. He hopped to a shoreline log and moved out onto the pond.

As he drew closer to the action his old friend Joe spotted him. Joe called from the shore to the two men balancing on logs.

"Hey, here comes our Charlie. Show them how it's done, you ol' rivercat!"

One of the birlers, turning to look at Charlie, missed his footing and tumbled into the pond. The men on shore roared with laughter.

"That's the way, Charlie. Take 'em by surprise!"

"Hey, I'm betting on you, Charlie!"

Charlie floated closer, and the remaining birler, Henry, butted his log against Charlie's, challenging him to a meet.

"Go get him, Charlie!" someone called from shore.

Henry was walking along the log, grinning from ear to ear. This was going to be the softest match he'd had, he was sure.

Charlie moved over onto Henry's log. Henry stopped walking and began shifting the log to keep his balance. Charlie moved easily as the log shifted, and the birling match was on.

The men cheered from shore.

"Birl 'im under, Charlie!"

"Five dollars on the cougar."

Henry did one tricky step after another. The birling was really going. Feet and cougar paws were flying. The men on shore cheered louder and louder.

Jess and the mill manager came out of the office, and the voices of the men reached them. They looked toward the pond just in time to see Henry sail off the log and drop into the water.

Jess grinned. "How about that for some fancy birling?"

The mill manager smiled, but something was obviously bothering him.

Jess gestured toward Charlie and called, "Come on, Charlie, come here!"

Charlie looked up. He was back on land, in the middle of the mill workers, who were loudly congratulating him. Like a celebrity, he gave them a nice big smile. Then he walked over toward Jess and the mill manager.

Jess laughed. "Crazy cat!"

The manager hesitated a moment, then said, "Jess, I hate to tell you this, but I can't stall any longer. He's got to go."

The smile disappeared from Jess's face.

"*Charlie?*"

The manager nodded. "Yes. The home office is putting on the heat . . . safety engineers . . . insurance company . . . everybody's getting in the act."

Charlie padded up and sat down in front of them. Jess stroked his head. The manager continued.

"Look, Jess, a full-sized cougar running loose around a sawmill — it really doesn't make much sense, does it?"

Jess was quiet, stroking Charlie's head. Then he looked directly at the manager.

"Okay," he sighed. "I'll keep him at home. Poor cat," he added, "he's sure gonna miss his friends around here."

The manager reached down and patted Charlie on the shoulder.

"His friends are sure going to miss Charlie."

CHARLIE MEETS A LADY

INSIDE a heavy wire enclosure, Charlie began his life as the lonesome cougar. Jess had done his best to make Charlie happy outdoors. He had rigged up a run for him next to the house. It gave Charlie room to move around comfortably and freely, but it was a cage, any way you looked at it.

Charlie still rode in the truck now and then. But Jess had been doing office work for weeks, so there wasn't much riding. Charlie spent the long hours pacing back and forth in his run, waiting for Jess to come home. It was sheer misery for the cougar. His whole life had revolved around the companionship of Jess Bradley and his friends at the Carbon County Mill.

The one bright spot in Charlie's day was when Jess came home from work. Charlie could hear the sound of Jess's truck long before the truck came into view. Like a faithful dog, he'd jump up on Jess the moment Jess opened the gate. From his throat would come the strange half-growl, half-mew which was his special sound of happiness.

Then the two of them would spend the rest of the evening together. Charlie always slept inside. Long ago he had outgrown Jess's bottom dresser drawer, but he still slept alongside it.

One evening Charlie lay sprawled out on the living room floor, washing himself. He was full of food and contentment. Jess came into the room whistling, all dressed up in a suit. Charlie's spirits immediately sagged. Jess walked to the front door, opened it, and gestured to Charlie.

"Come on, Charlie, time to put out the cat. C'mon, buddy, outside."

Charlie slowly rose and padded over to Jess. He sat down and looked up.

"It makes a long lonesome day, doesn't it, Charlie-boy?" Jess gave Charlie a couple of pats on the back and urged him outside. He closed the door, then led Charlie to the enclosure. Charlie reluctantly walked in, and Jess latched the gate.

"See you later, fella," Jess said. "Keep an eye on things." Jess walked away, then glanced back. Charlie was sitting just inside the gate, looking utterly dejected. "Maybe we'll both have some company around here someday. Cheer up, boy." He waved, got into the pickup, and drove off in the late evening light.

Charlie stood for a while at the gate, his eyes following the pickup as it moved away. When he could no longer see the truck, he lay down. This was not the first night that Jess had left Charlie alone. But as it turned out, it was to be the last.

As Charlie lay dejectedly with his head on his fore-paws a new, yet strangely familiar, scent reached him. Slowly he lifted his head, his nostrils busily sampling the air. He rose and stared up toward the mountains.

High among the rimrocks, another cougar was on the prowl. It was a young unattached female, wilderness-bred, and out to see the world. She paused on a ridge, sil-houetted against the rising moon.

Charlie didn't see her, but he knew she was there. He paced his enclosure nervously, swiping at the heavy wire with his powerful paws. He even tried to reach the outside latch, but the wire openings were too small for his big paws. He looked upward and scanned the pos-sibilities.

Under the eaves where the wire had been nailed to the side of the house was a good-sized opening. Charlie leaped toward it, clung to the wire, and clawed his way to the opening. He stuck his head through, twisting and squirming. Seconds later his whole body was free. He leaped to the ground and landed, then ran toward the wooded hillside.

The female, padding along the top of a huge boul-der, stopped and looked down the hill. Charlie had just rounded the boulder. He looked up and came to a sud-den halt.

Up to now, Charlie had seen many things unknown to other cougars. But he'd never seen what to other cou-gars is commonplace — another cougar!

The female cougar sat on her haunches and cocked

her head to one side with friendly interest. She weighed about a hundred and ten pounds. She was four feet long and about two feet high — much smaller than Charlie, although they were about the same age. She was a very pale slate gray color, except for the tips of her ears and tail, which were a darker gray. Not knowing what else to do, Charlie bared his teeth in a smile.

The female returned his smile.

They touched noses.

The female hopped down from the boulder and bounded away. Charlie was right behind her. They chased each other and rolled and tussled in the underbrush. The female climbed a tree and leaped down in mock attack. Then it was Charlie's turn. They romped

their way deeper and deeper into the wilderness. Charlie forgot all about his loneliness.

Cougars have remarkable ground-covering ability. By the time the first rays of the rising sun glinted through the trees, the two of them had covered nearly thirty miles.

Now Charlie began to think about breakfast. So did his companion. She was mountain-born and she knew what to do about food. When something stirred in the brush, she moved away from Charlie and quietly crept toward it. Suddenly a rabbit broke through the other side of the brush and hopped into the meadow.

The female crashed through the brush in hot pursuit. Charlie padded through the brush behind the chase. He saw her pounce on the rabbit just before it reached the cover of the woods.

Charlie bounded across the meadow to where the female lay feeding in the underbrush. Charlie had no doubt that she'd be willing to share her food. He confidently trotted into the bushes to enjoy breakfast with his new friend.

The female whirled around and snarled. Rushing at him, she clawed him first with one paw, then with the other. Charlie squalled and stumbled backward. The female followed for a few steps, snarling all the time. Charlie flew out of the brush and up the nearest tree!

Wilderness life was full of surprises. For one thing, breakfasts ran away. For another, friends didn't share their food. These were things Charlie had never before in his life experienced. And to top it all, here he was — treed by a little lady who was telling him what to do!

FISHING WITH A BEAR

CHARLIE didn't dare climb down from the tree until his female friend had left. He walked around the brush, sniffing, but she had done a thorough job on the rabbit. There wasn't a morsel left.

Charlie sat down dejectedly. He was exhausted from his all-night walk and very hungry. Worst of all, as he scanned the unfamiliar territory, he realized that he didn't know the way home.

He stretched out, rested his head on his forepaws, and sighed. Slowly his eyes began to close.

When he awakened, it was night again. Charlie sat up and looked about uncertainly.

He headed across the meadow and wandered through the brush. He climbed over and down a mountain which was familiar to him. Somehow the lonesome cougar was retracing his steps. In spite of his hunger,

Charlie's greatest need was still to find his way back to Jess. But he was a long way from the homestead. And more than distance lay between him and Jess — he was hungry.

All night he chased various small animals, vainly trying to fend for himself. By the evening of the next day Charlie had been outwitted by a number of rabbits, a raccoon, and several kinds of birds. If any of his first hunting expeditions had been successful, he might have gone on to bigger things. As it was, he didn't, and his road to survival took a strange twist.

The moon was up full when Charlie arrived at a creek, footsore, weak, and weary. He flopped down on the bank and drank deeply of the cool water. Charlie was in serious trouble. His food problem could no longer be solved, even temporarily, by drinking water.

Suddenly, a short distance away, a loud splashing noise interrupted Charlie's drinking. He started as if to run, then changed his mind. Hunger had made Charlie bold. He began to stalk in a low-bellied movement toward the sound. He was going to eat something, and he didn't care much what it was. He crept up a high rocky bank, eased forward silently, and peered down.

There was a big black bear splashing about in the creek below. Charlie sat very still, watching. He was certainly hungry enough to eat a bear, but he just didn't know where to begin!

Fortunately the bear came up with an alternative. It had been fishing and had caught a good-sized salmon. The bear flipped the fish ashore and lumbered out of the creek after it. But Charlie made his move too and pounced down the bank. At the same moment, Charlie

and the bear arrived at the spot where the fish was lying. The bear gave a mighty growl and took a swipe at Charlie. But Charlie's need was greater than any fear he might have of the bear. Charlie snarled and slapped back.

The bear and the cougar then did a lot of bluffing, but Charlie had learned a few food-swiping tricks from a dog named Chainsaw. Fortunately one of those tricks paid off.

Charlie faked a dash into the creek, and the clumsy bear turned to follow him. As soon as the bear turned, Charlie leaped back, grabbed the salmon, and ran for the brush. He moved like lightning, and the bear didn't even attempt to go after him. Instead it waded back into the water. There were plenty more salmon in the creek.

From a vantage point above the creek, Charlie lowered his head to eat. The fish hadn't been easy to get and wasn't too tasty, but it was food. Charlie gulped it down and then watched the bear catching another salmon. Charlie was still hungry, and the bear was still catching food. Now Charlie knew exactly what to do.

CHARLIE LEARNS HIS ROLE

DAYS later, Charlie still sat on the shore, watching the bear fish in the stream. He had become completely dependent on the bear for his food. As for the bear, he had resigned himself to fishing for two mouths. He and Charlie didn't even squabble any more.

One morning Charlie took up his usual spectator position, but the bear was nowhere to be seen. Charlie paced along the water's edge and scanned the bank above. Suddenly he spotted his provider, comfortably snoozing under a tree. Charlie approached and snarled impatiently. But the bear continued to sleep because he had already had a hearty breakfast in a blueberry patch.

Charlie moved to the creek and peered into the water. A salmon glided by, right under his nose. Charlie pounced into the water. He chased the slippery salmon all over the stream, splashing and sliding and slipping.

The chase ended in deep water, and the salmon escaped easily. Charlie had to swim ashore.

He padded back to his waiting station at the creek's edge. To his surprise, the bear had gone. Although Charlie didn't know it, the bear was heading for a different food supply. Charlie was on his own again, as hungry and inexperienced as ever.

He made his way to a grassy hillside, lay down, and took stock of his surroundings. In the meadow below, Charlie caught sight of a bobcat, stalking low in the grass. Charlie sat up attentively and watched. The bobcat was much smaller than Charlie, about as big as a medium-sized dog.

Something skittered through the grass, and the bobcat broke, pounced, and captured a meadow mouse. Charlie watched the bobcat until he had finished feeding. The cougar knew from experience that there was no sharing with another cat. He also knew that food of some sort was available down there. Charlie started down to scare away the bobcat and take over the field. But he didn't even have to try. The bobcat spotted Charlie, gave a frightened hiss, and ran into the woods.

Charlie hadn't seen many animals run from him. He just stood there and watched until the bobcat was out of sight. Now he had a clear field all to himself. He wasted no time.

There was movement in the grass just inches away. His head snapped around, and a mouse scooted through the grass. He pounced. The mouse darted into a clump of grass. Charlie bounded all about the meadow. He leaped, he pounced, missed, and pounced again. When he finally made a catch, he was winded. But he'd made his first kill, and there would be many more. Charlie was right in the middle of a meadow full of mice.

For hours Charlie stalked, pounced, missed, chased, and pounced again. In due time he became a master hunter — of mice!

It was a lot of work for such small returns. Nevertheless, from these meager beginnings, Charlie was finally learning the art of hunting.

For weeks Charlie lived on small game. Then one day at the edge of a grassy clearing, he saw a deer feeding. He charged. The deer ran for cover, but it was too late. At last, Charlie had assumed his rightful role.

Throughout the winter and into spring, the way of the wilderness became more and more Charlie's way. And just as he had learned that he was born to hunt, he also learned that he was hunted.

One spring day as he lay sleeping on a flower-covered hillside, Charlie was wakened by the howling and baying of hounds. A bounty hunter was on his trail. Instantly he was awake. For a moment conflicting impulses fought within him. His urge for headlong flight fought against his instinct for caution. In his confusion he ran downhill and into an open field. The hounds and the hunter immediately spotted him.

A terrible fear urged Charlie to fantastic speed. Across a stump-dotted clearing he raced toward a nearby river. The hounds, still baying in pursuit, were losing ground.

Charlie hesitated for a moment at the river's edge. At this spot logs were tumbling into the river down a chute. Then as the cry of the dog pack and the sound of

horse's hooves drew nearer, Charlie made a long leap. But not long enough. Instead of landing on the other side, Charlie landed on a log!

For Charlie log riding was an old, familiar sport. It worked out fine. He could keep moving and catch his breath at the same time.

Charlie looked back. The hounds were at the water's edge, barking by the log chute. The bounty hunter reined up behind the dogs. He figured the cougar had somehow reached the other side.

After some consideration the hunter decided not to swim across on his horse. The river was deep. He and the hounds turned back in the direction from which they had come.

Charlie, out on the river on his log, was picking up speed. The river seemed to drop. Charlie clawed at the log desperately. At breakneck speed he traveled for several miles, hanging on for dear life. Then suddenly the river leveled off again.

Charlie found himself in a quiet mill pond, floating easily among many logs. As he passed close to shore he leaped to the bank. He swayed unsteadily as he stood at last on solid ground. He looked about. Familiar scents greeted him. And through the dusk of evening he could make out a road above the bank.

His memory stirred and tugged. Slowly, then faster, he ran up the shallow bank. There it was for sure — Potlatch's cafe and the mill office! Everyone had gone home, but that made no difference to Charlie.

He'd been a lost and lonesome cougar long enough. At last he was home.

CHARLIE'S HOMECOMING

CHARLIE ran to the mill office. It was closed for the night. He circled the building, trying to locate Jess's scent. It wasn't there.

Then another well-remembered scent reached Charlie, reminding him of his empty stomach. With a final glance at the mill office, he padded over to Potlatch's cafe. He sat down outside the kitchen door, waiting as he'd often done before. No one came. He called with his old friendly growl. Still no Potlatch. Charlie got up and sniffed around the door sill. He moved along the building, sniffing as he went. Near the front of the restaurant, he stopped and looked up. There was a window, covered only by a loose-fitting screen.

Charlie sized up the distance to the window, crouched, and leaped. He sailed into the restaurant and landed on the floor, carrying the screen with him. Startled by the crash it made, he leaped onto the counter. From there he surveyed the empty dining room through the dim light. He spotted the doorway leading to the kitchen. He moved carefully along the counter, dropped to the floor, and entered the kitchen.

The smell of food was everywhere, but Charlie couldn't find any. It was all safely stored in the refrigerator or in cans.

Charlie sniffed at the refrigerator door and pawed it. No luck. He padded away and pushed through a partly open door into a small pantry. It was lined with shelves of canned goods.

A mouse trap, baited with a short strip of bacon, lay under a pantry shelf. Charlie went for the bacon, and the trap snapped shut, stinging his nose. As he jumped back he hit the door. It slammed shut, and the spring latch clicked and locked.

Charlie looked around, terrified. The sudden confinement in such a small place sent him into panic. He leaped and clawed up the walls in a frantic effort to escape the cramped, windowless cubicle.

He pounced at the shelves, wreaking havoc amid Potlatch's staples. Boxes, cans, bottles, and jars came tumbling down. He even ripped down some of the shelves in his utter panic.

Poor Charlie! He spent the whole night pacing in a tight circle amid all the debris. What was worse, there was still nothing to eat. He nervously stepped around in broken bottles of catsup, vinegar, and salad dressing. It was all like a terrible nightmare.

The start of the day at the mill was usually a dull, standard routine. But this morning was to be different, in a way that would be long remembered.

Potlatch arrived at the cafe with Chainsaw at his heels. As he started to unlock the door Chainsaw suddenly stopped and sniffed the air.

Potlatch looked down at him.

"Hold your horses, dog. Ain't nothin' cooking yet."

Chainsaw growled, then took off around the corner of the building. Potlatch looked mildly surprised, but shrugged and went on inside the cafe. He left the main door open and closed the screen door behind him. Before he could turn around he had two customers. One of them was Henry, Charlie's old pal from his river days.

Henry said, "Mornin', Potlatch. How's the coffee?"

Potlatch shook his head.

"You guys'll have to wait. I haven't even plugged in the coffee urn yet." He went behind the counter. "Everybody's sure in a hurry this morning."

"Hey, Potlatch," said Henry. "What's your window screen doing on the floor?"

Potlatch looked up at the window, then at the screen on the floor. He glanced quickly around the dining room. Everything else seemed in place. He scratched his head.

"I don't know, Henry. Must've been the wind. How 'bout you putting it back for me while I'm making your coffee?"

Henry chuckled. "Sure gotta go through a lot around here for a little service."

Around the side of the restaurant, Chainsaw had started up a frenzy of growls and barks. Inside the pantry Charlie, still pacing his circle, heard the muffled sounds of Chainsaw's familiar barking. Charlie tensed.

Chainsaw, scenting Charlie, scratched at the kitchen door with more yelping and growling. In a frenzy he ran around to the front door and barked and whined at the screen.

Henry and the other workman were just starting to drink their coffee.

"What's the matter with that mutt?" Henry complained. "Can't a man have a simple cup of coffee around here any more?"

Potlatch came from behind the counter.

"I dunno what's eatin' him this morning!" he said. He opened the screen door and started to say something, but Chainsaw darted between his legs, barking wildly. He shot straight through the restaurant toward the pantry.

Potlatch went after him and found him growling and clawing at the pantry door.

"What's the matter with you, Chainsaw?" Potlatch said irritably. "There's nothing in there but —" He pushed the door open.

Charlie came hurtling out, flattening Potlatch under his leap. He raced wildly out of the kitchen and leaped onto the counter, scaring Henry and the workman half to death.

They dropped to the floor and covered their heads.

Charlie continued his mad flight across the counter, scattering sugar bowls and salt and pepper shakers in his wake. Chainsaw came yowling out of the kitchen, and Charlie bolted right through the screen door.

Potlatch erupted from the kitchen, waving a meat cleaver. He yelled at Henry and the workman.

"It's Charlie! He's gone bad! C'mon, we gotta get him!"

The two men scrambled up from the floor and rushed after Potlatch. Henry grabbed an ax out of his pickup and the other workman seized a heavy length of chain. Charlie had disappeared around a building, but Chainsaw's incessant barking led the three men in his direction. Suddenly Chainsaw's barks turned to frightened whimpers, and he came running back around the corner of the building at top speed, with Charlie in pursuit. They were headed straight for Potlatch.

Potlatch pulled up and wildly threw the cleaver at Charlie, yelling, "He's gone bad! He's a killer!"

Charlie swerved, spun around, and headed toward the mill office. Potlatch retrieved his cleaver, and the three men raced after Charlie.

By a not-quite-forgotten habit, Charlie had run for the mill office. But at this early hour only the manager was there. When he heard all the commotion, he leaned across his desk and looked out of the window. Immediately he yanked open his desk drawer, pulled out a revolver, and headed for the door.

Charlie had nearly reached the office when the manager burst out of the door. Potlatch was yelling, "Killer!" and "Gone bad!" The mill manager fired a couple of hasty shots. Charlie swerved again and dashed off in another direction. He ran wildly across the yard.

Now there were four men after him. Another shot rang in the air, and Charlie looked about frantically for some means of escape. He raced toward the storage shed, his terror growing as the violent sounds of his pursuers grew.

By now several of the mill workers had come out of the mill and had joined in the chase. They carried wrenches and pickaxes, hammers, chains, pocket knives — anything they could lay their hands on. Charlie's circle of friends had turned into a ring of killers.

Blindly Charlie ran through the storage shed between the tall stacks of lumber. The men had now organized their pursuit and were spreading out.

Someone spotted Charlie and shouted, "There he is — get him!"

Charlie dashed into a three-sided "box canyon" between stacks. He realized his mistake and turned to get out. But Potlatch and Henry had moved into the entrance and stood in his path with raised weapons.

"We got him!" they both yelled. "Here he is!"

Charlie was trapped in the box canyon. Every cougar instinct in him came alive. He was frightened, cornered, and dangerous.

Other men arrived at the entryway now, among them a workman carrying a long pike pole. He prodded Charlie with the pole. Charlie snarled viciously, swiped at the pole, and knocked it out of the workman's hands. Henry stepped up and drew back his ax. Finally Charlie turned on his former friends. He lunged forward, snarling and striking with his paws.

Henry threw the ax. It whizzed past Charlie and the blade struck deep into the wall. Potlatch moved cautiously forward with the cleaver. Charlie tensed himself. These two, once friends, were now mortal enemies.

At this moment the mill manager shouldered his way through the crowd.

"You'd better let me handle this," he said. He raised his gun and aimed at Charlie's head, right between the eyes. . . .

THE END OF
THE LONESOME TRAIL

JESS arrived at the mill in the midst of the uproar. A workman ran by, waving a hammer in the air.

"Hey!" called Jess from his pickup truck. "What's up?"

The workman didn't stop. He just called over his shoulder, "We got him now! He's a killer!" and kept running.

Jess was seized with sudden alarm. "Who's a killer?" he yelled, but the workman kept going and didn't answer.

Jess slammed down on the accelerator and drove at top speed toward the shed. Somehow he knew what they were talking about. He feared also that Charlie was in terrible trouble. Jess only hoped he wouldn't be too late.

Screeching to a stop at the storage shed, he jumped from the truck. The men were all over the shed, blocking the passageways. He pushed his way through, shouting, "Get outta the way! That's Charlie back there! Let me through!"

He arrived breathless at the spot where Charlie was trapped. The tight, angry knot of men moved resentfully aside. Jess plunged through to the mill manager.

"Hold it!" he cried. He dove at the manager's gun hand. "That's Charlie!"

Charlie snarled threateningly.

"Not the same Charlie you knew, Jess," said the manager.

Jess was unconvinced. "Look," he said. "He's scared half to death. Let me handle this."

The mill manager hesitated, looking at Jess, then at Charlie.

"Okay, it's your hide." He stepped back, but kept the gun aimed at Charlie.

Jess turned to Charlie. The cougar snarled again.

"Okay, Charlie," Jess crooned. "Now just take it easy, boy." He turned to a workman. "Let me have that chain, Slim."

The workman handed over the chain and edged his way back into the crowd.

Jess spoke softly, "It's going to be all right, Charlie."

Charlie snarled again, but he seemed less menacing.

"That's the way, fella." Jess eased closer and closer. He wanted to give Charlie plenty of time to recognize him.

"Relax, cat, don't let me down now, Charlie."

Jess stopped a couple of feet from him. The cougar

was still wary, but he no longer snarled.

Jess smiled, "It's old home week, buddy. Jess and Charlie."

Charlie cocked his head to the side. Then he let out a pitiful wail. It was his old kitten cry for help, grown gruffer with age. He moved toward Jess. Jess knelt and gently stroked his head and ears.

"Hi, Charlie. It's been a long time."

The workers watched in wonder. Jess looped the chain around Charlie's neck, stroked him again, and stood up.

"Come on, fella. Let's get out of here."

He led Charlie toward the now quiet crowd. They parted silently to make room. Fear had turned them into a violent mob a short time before. Perhaps it was they who had "turned bad" and not the terrified cougar.

Jess and Charlie were together again, but it wasn't for long. In fact, a few days later Charlie had his last ride in Jess's pickup.

Seated in the back, the wind blowing in his face, Charlie viewed the forested mountain country as Jess drove along the big highway. Next to Jess sat a pretty young lady who had come along for the ride.

She turned and tapped the rear window playfully in front of Charlie's face. Charlie grinned at her.

She turned to Jess.

"Don't look so grim. Charlie will be safe and happy at the sanctuary."

Jess smiled.

"Sure — he might even find a nice girl like you."

Jess had finally realized that a cougar was born to a

taller land and a wider sky and had no place in the world of people. He had decided to give Charlie his natural cougar life — much as he loved Charlie and wanted to keep him.

They pulled off the highway onto a dirt road. The sign at the entrance read, "National Wildlife Sanctuary. No Hunting."

More than a thousand square miles of primitive wilderness stretched ahead of Charlie. No dogs, guns, or bounty hunters. This was Charlie's new home.

Jess climbed out of the truck and motioned to Charlie.

"Come on, fella."

Charlie leaped from the back of the truck. The girl handed Jess a large brown paper bag.

"I'll just walk him a little way and come right back," Jess said.

The girl leaned over and said, "Jess, are you sure?"

Jess grinned.

"You bet! Besides, in all that wilderness, I just know Charlie's going to find the right girl too." Then he and Charlie walked into the woods.

After they had gone some distance, Jess stopped. He reached into the paper bag and pulled out a large hunk of raw meat. Charlie sat and looked up at him.

"I got a feeling you'll be able to take care of yourself around here, fella. Just don't go 'round grinning like that, though!"

He dropped the meat in front of the cougar. Charlie pounced on it, then stretched out with it between his forepaws.

"Well — so long, old buddy." Jess turned and

walked back toward the road. A moment later he stopped and looked back. Charlie was busy feeding. Jess smiled.

"That's your last free meal, pal. Enjoy it." Jess waved and walked on.

A few minutes later, the pickup motor started. Charlie looked up from the meat curiously. He turned his head to the side, listening as the truck backed up on the road to turn around. Then he jumped up and raced toward the road. When he got there, Jess had pulled away onto the highway. Charlie watched as the truck drove out of sight.

Then Charlie raced back to the spot where he had left the meat. He picked it up. Suddenly he dropped the meat and sniffed the air. In a flash he was off, running into the woods.

When he came upon the female cougar, she was seated in the middle of a clearing, washing herself. Charlie loped over to her, and they touched noses.

Charlie had found his girl sooner than Jess could have guessed. She was of the slate-colored variety, slim and sleek. She might even have been the same young female that Charlie had romped with in the moonlight, many moons before.

The two cougars padded across the clearing together, shoulders rubbing, and disappeared into the trees. Charlie was not going to be lonely again.